THE DUCK
WHO
LOVED PUDDLES

Written by Michael J. Pellowski

Illustrated by Diane Paterson

Troll Associates

Library of Congress Cataloging in Publication Data

Pellowski, Michael.
   The duck who loved puddles.

   Summary: A little duck looks everywhere on the farm
for a wet place to splash, but all the water seems to be
intended for someone else.
   [1. Ducks—Fiction. 2. Domestic animals—Fiction.
3. Farm life—Fiction] I. Paterson, Diane, 1946-   ill.
II. Title.
PZ7.P3656Du   1986   [E]   85-14058
ISBN 0-8167-0578-X (lib. bdg.)
ISBN 0-8167-0579-8 (pbk.)

THE DUCK
WHO
LOVED PUDDLES

Puddles was a little duck.
He belonged to Farmer Dodd.
How did Puddles get his name?
This is how!

Puddles loved to splash.
Splish! Splash!
"The more puddles, the better!"
said the little duck.

Puddles was Farmer Dodd's pet
duck. Puddles lived on a farm. A
farm is a good place for a pet
duck—especially one who likes
to be wet.

He splashed in puddles here.
He splashed in puddles there.
He splashed in every puddle he
could find. What a wet little
duck Puddles was!

What makes puddles on a farm?
Rain makes puddles. But
sometimes it does not rain.
Sometimes there are no puddles.
Without rain a farm is a dry
place.

9

Puddles the duck did not like to be dry. He liked to be wet. "Where can I splash?" said Puddles.

Puddles looked for a wet place.
He looked and looked. Poor little
Puddles! All of the places that
once were wet, now were dry.
Puddles was not happy. A dry
duck is not a happy duck.

11

"I must find a new wet place,"
said Puddles. "I must find water
to splash in. But where can I
find water?"

Puddles went to the barn. Cows
lived there. Puddles liked the
cows. The cows liked Puddles.

"Hi, cow," said Puddles. "I am looking for water. All of the old places are dry."

The cow looked at Puddles.
"It has been very dry," said the
cow. "But there is water by the
barn. It is in a tub. Farmer
Dodd put a tub of water by the
barn."

"Oh boy!" cried Puddles. "Water!"
Away ran Puddles. He ran to the
tub of water by the barn.

SPLASH! Into the tub went
Puddles. Splash! Splash! Oh,
what good wet water! Puddles
splashed and splashed!

17

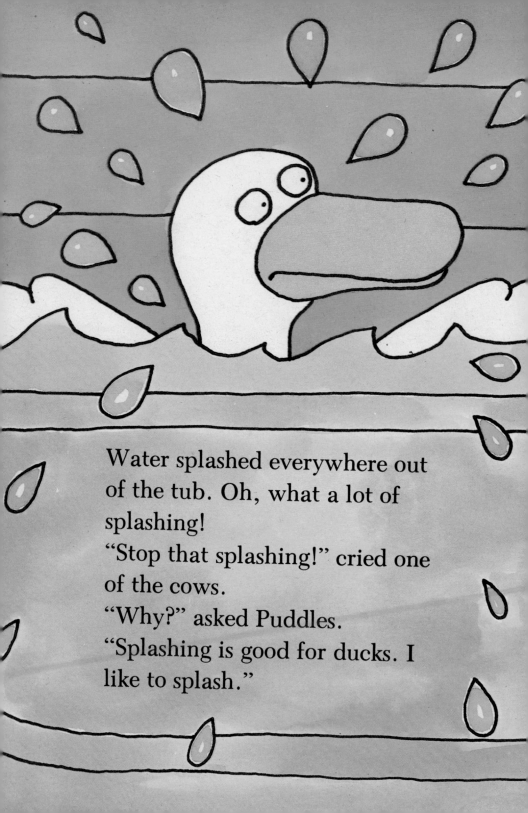

Water splashed everywhere out
of the tub. Oh, what a lot of
splashing!
"Stop that splashing!" cried one
of the cows.
"Why?" asked Puddles.
"Splashing is good for ducks. I
like to splash."

The cow said, "I want to drink.
This water is not for ducks. It is
for cows. It is not for splashing.
It is for drinking."

Puddles stopped.
"Drinking water?" cried
Puddles. "Not splashing water!
Cow water? Not duck water! I
must find a new wet place."

Puddles got out. The cow drank
out of the tub. Away went the
duck. Poor little Puddles! He
was unhappy. A dry duck is not
a happy duck.

"Where to look?" said Puddles.
"Where? Where? Where?"
Puddles looked by the brook.
No wet places there. The brook
was dry.

22

Puddles went to the pond.
No water there. Away went the
unhappy little duck.

Puddles went to see Farmer
Dodd's dog. The dog lived in a
doghouse. By the doghouse was
a little dish. In the dish was
water.

"Oh boy!" cried Puddles.
Into the dog's dish went Puddles.
Splash! Splash! Splash!

The dog was in the doghouse.
"What is that splashing?" he
asked.
Out he went.
"A duck in my dish!" he cried.
"Out! Out! Out! I do not want a
duck in my water."

Puddles looked at the dog. The
dog was not happy.
"I will go," said Puddles.
And away he went.

Poor little Puddles! He could not splash in the cows' tub. He could not splash in the brook. He could not splash in the pond. No splashing in the dog's dish either. Where could he find water?

"Farmer Dodd has water in his
house," said Puddles.
"I am Farmer Dodd's pet duck.
I will go in the farmhouse."

Into the farmhouse went the little duck. He looked for a wet place. He found one. Where? In the kitchen sink! Dishes were in the water.

Oh, what a silly duck! Ducks
cannot splash in the kitchen
sink. A sink is for washing
dishes. A sink is not for ducks.

"A new wet place!" cried
Puddles. Into the sink he went.
Splash! Splash! Splash!
Puddles splashed in the sink.

32

Mrs. Dodd was in the
farmhouse.
"What is that splashing?" she
asked.
Mrs. Dodd went to look.

What did Mrs. Dodd see? She saw a wet duck in her kitchen sink!

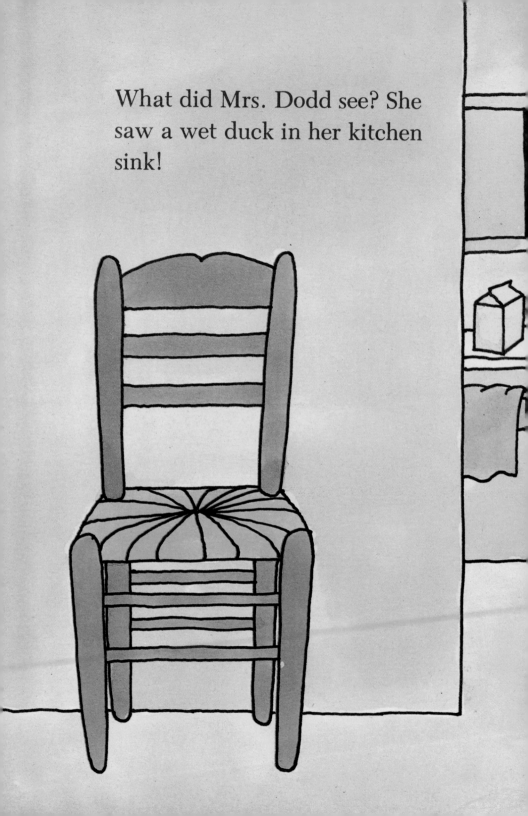

"Puddles is in there!" she cried.
"A pet duck in with the dishes!
Oh no! Go, duck! Go! Out!
Out! Out!"

35

Puddles heard Mrs. Dodd. Out
of the sink he went. Away he
ran. But he did not go out of the
house.

Puddles found a new wet place.
It was a place for baths. The
place was a bathtub. The
bathtub was filled with water.
It was Farmer Dodd's bath.

"Oh boy!" cried Puddles. "A good place for splashing. It is not as big as the pond. It is not as big as the brook. But it is a good place."

38

SPLASH! Into the bathtub went
Puddles. Happily, he splashed!

Farmer Dodd went in for his
bath. What did he find? In his
tub was a duck. A duck was
splashing in his bath water.
Farmer Dodd was not happy.

"Puddles, you silly duck!" he
cried. "Out of my tub! Out of
my house! Out! Out! Out!"

Puddles got out in a hurry! He ran by Farmer Dodd. He ran by Mrs. Dodd. Out of the house he ran.

Poor Puddles! No wet places in the house. No wet places out of the house. No more water. No more splashing. What an unhappy little duck.

"Without rain, a farm is a very dry place," said Puddles. "Dry places are not good for ducks. Ducks like to be wet. Ducks like rain."

Rain? Sometimes it does not
rain. But sometimes it does rain.
And rain it did!
"Oh boy! Rain!" cried Puddles
happily.

It rained and rained. Water in
the brook. Water in the pond.
All of the old places were wet
again.

Puddles splashed in the brook.
He splashed and splashed.

Puddles splashed in the pond.
He splashed and splashed.
Puddles was a wet duck once
again—and a wet duck is a
happy duck!